ALSO

Children's Books

C is for Cowboy: A Wyoming Alphabet

The Magic Box

Four Wheels West: A Wyoming Number Book
Western Writers Spur Award nominee

V is for Venus Flytrap: A Plant Alphabet

My Teacher Dances on the Desk
Delaware Diamonds Book List
Children's Choice Award

Dee and the Mammoth
Wyoming State Historical Society Award for Best Fiction
National Book Festival in Washington, D.C.

Little Wyoming

Little Hawaii

My Veggie Friends

Celebrate the Season—Twelve Short Stories for Advent and Christmas
"Lighting Up the Darkness"

Bruce Coville's Book of Nightmares
"The Hand"

MG/Pre-teen Books

Chicken Soup for the Preteen Soul: 101 Stories of Changes, Choices and Growing Up for Kids
"You'll Be Good for Him"

Secret of the Black Widow
Wyoming Indian Paintbrush Award nominee

Inside the Clown

Falling Stars

Booger

Angel's Landing

Is It True?
National Book Festival in Washington, D.C.

What Did You Say?

Snap
EVVY Award

Wedge of Fear
EVVY Award

Adult Poetry

Prairie Parcels

A Wyoming State of Mind

More Than Four Seasons

ICE CAVE MYSTERY

Eugene M. Gagliano

Crystal Publishing, LLC
Fort Collins, Colorado

Ice Cave Mystery

2023 © COPYRIGHT Eugene M. Gagliano
2023 © COVER COPYRIGHT Crystal Publishing, LLC

Edited by Malory Wood and Patricia Phillips
Cover and interior design by Lotus Design, lotusdesign.biz

This is a work of fiction. Names, characters, places, and incidents either are the product of the author's imagination or are used fictitiously. Any resemblance to actual persons, living or dead, events, or locales is entirely coincidental.

Published by Crystal Publishing, LLC
Fort Collins, Colorado

ISBN: 978-1-942624-79-0

Library of Congress Control Number: 2023939363

ALL RIGHTS RESERVED

Printed in the U.S.A.

For Patricia Landy who believed in me as a writer with 100 percent support.

NOTHING BUT TROUBLE

"Hello? Who's there?"

Alarmed, Chad whirled around. He searched the surrounding trees. Nothing was there except the waxy green leaves of the cottonwoods shimmering in the late afternoon sun. He felt something or...someone staring at him. Chad froze in place when a branch snapped. His ears pricked up while he frantically surveyed the landscape. Nothing appeared on the path behind him. Probably just a squirrel. He brushed away the thought and continued up the game trail, which veered to the left and turned into a path bordering a wide creek.

Stepping onto a large granite boulder, he sat down and allowed his gaze to follow the swirling water of Clear Creek downstream. The splashing diamond droplets sparkled. He took a deep breath, relishing the scent of warm pine needles.

Chad traced the lines in the rock, and his thoughts drifted. They reminded him of the veins in Grandpa's hands. He missed Grandpa. It was 1890. Two summers had passed since his family had left Indiana.

Two-year-old Becky, his only sister, had died from cholera along the Oregon Trail. It still felt like a bad dream, and his heart still ached for her.

Since then, he had made a new friend, Aubrey, whose mother

still wore the scars from the fire that killed her husband. Chad had grown to love her little brother, Jesse, but like Becky, he was now gone, and that added to his ache.

Already weeks had passed since Jesse became sick and died. His heart still longed for both Becky and Jessie, and he knew Aubrey still pined for her little brother. Yet life went on, like the creek that paid no attention to the boulders, fallen trees, and other obstacles in its path.

An uneasy feeling swept over him. This was no squirrel. Maybe a mountain lion watched from the dappled green shade. He should go home, but he overheard an old man and a soldier talking. In his mind, he imagined the old-timer with his sweat-stained hat. Chad wanted to discover for himself if the old man told the truth. What if he'd only made up the story? No, it must be true.

Ma and Pa took the wagon to Fort McKinney to sell vegetables and eggs. While the store manager checked over the beans, Chad studied the glass candy jars. A young soldier, Corporal William Wilson from Company 1, Ninth Cavalry stood chatting with an old man near the pickle barrel.

"I've heard tell of it," the gray-bearded man said. "The Ice Cave's nothing but trouble, as far as I know." He spit some chew into the spittoon. "Can't say as I ever come across it myself, but I know it's pretty well hid."

"Is it far from the fort?" The soldier leaned against the wooden counter of the mercantile.

"I reckon not, but I'd be careful if I was you. A mess of bears and a mountain lion or two been spotted along the creek."

Chad just had to find the Ice Cave, but what if a bear stood watching him from behind a clump of chokecherry bushes? A swarm of gnats flew into his face. He sputtered and brushed them aside with his arm.

A startled mule deer headed up the mountainside. Something must have spooked it. Chad stared into the trees. Then, he picked up a small granite rock and stood ready to throw it.

"Don't!" A familiar voice shouted. "It's me."

"Aubrey! What are you doing here?"

"I followed you," Aubrey said, approaching Chad from behind some pine trees. "I saw you from far away." She wiped some brown spruce needles off her green gingham dress sleeve.

"Where're you going?"

"I'm looking for somethin'."

"What?"

Chad frowned. "It's a secret. I didn't want anyone to know."

"Not even me?" Aubrey scowled. "I thought you were my best friend."

"You are, but this could be dangerous." Chad tossed the rock into the creek. "I don't want to cause you no harm."

Aubrey shook her red braids in defiance. "I can take care of myself, Chad Ryan. Now tell me. What's the secret?"

Chad sighed. "You're too stubborn."

"And you're being silly. You can trust me."

"Alright. Promise you won't tell anyone?"

"I promise." Aubrey crossed her heart and stared at Chad.

"I'm looking for the Ice Cave." Chad brushed some more gnats away. "I heard some guys talking about it. It's supposed to be close by. They said it was nothin' but trouble."

"Why would it be trouble?"

Chad shrugged his shoulders. "That's what I want to find out."

Chad and Aubrey followed the trail along the creek. The sound of gurgling water and the hum of bees brightened the day. The clacking sound of a kingfisher searching for trout along the creek caught his attention. Chad looked for the blue and white bird, easy to spot because of its long beak.

The creek opened into a meadow filled with yellow flowers. The chirping sound of birds surrounded Chad and Aubrey.

"Aubrey, look. See the owl?"

He pointed to the great horned owl perched on the skeleton of a large pine tree. Suddenly, it gracefully lifted into the air without a sound. The large bird flew off into a grove of towering pine.

"I wish I could fly like that," Chad said, staring off into the blue. "Oh yuck!"

"What? What is it?"

"I just stepped in somethin' mushy. It looks like fresh bear scat."

Chad searched the large clumps of chokecherries that grew scattered over the meadow. He spotted something black moving in the bushes several yards away. He slowly backed up and tapped Aubrey on the shoulder. He motioned for her to back away toward the path at the edge of the meadow. Chad knew he was upwind from the bear. Bears have poor eyesight, so it probably hadn't seen or smelled him yet.

When they reached the safety of the trees along the path, he gave a long sigh. He didn't want to tangle with a hungry bear.

"Let's go. It's gettin' late. We can come back another time,"

Chad said.

Finding the Ice Cave would have to wait.

QUESTIONS

The next day, after Chad had finished milking Bertie, the family cow, fed the chickens, and completed his other chores, he headed to the Foster farm to get Aubrey. It was going to be another hot summer day. Chad saw a flash of red fox dart behind some tall grasses. Off in the distance, the Big Horn Mountains appeared like giants rising from the prairie. Snow still capped the tallest peaks, which shone brilliantly in the sun. The thought of snow sounded good today, but he was glad winter had long since passed. He could hear the tapping sound of a woodpecker in a dead pine tree but couldn't see it.

The smell of fresh-baked bread greeted him as he approached the Foster cabin. The widow, Mrs. Foster, waved to Chad as he opened the front gate.

"Hi, Chad," she said, turning the unscarred side of her face toward him. "Looks like it's gonna be another hot day," the widow said as she continued to hang some laundry on the clothesline.

"I can smell your bread," Chad said.

"I thought it best to get it done before the heat of the day," Mrs. Foster said. "How's your ma?"

"She's fine. Said to say hello."

Aubrey stepped out of the cabin, cuddling Sunny, the little

yellow kitten Chad had given her after Jesse died. "Hi, Chad. I'm ready to go." She put Sunny down on the ground. "He's the cutest thing, Chad. I love to watch him play." Aubrey tied her blue gingham bonnet.

"Did you finish all your chores?" the widow asked.

"Yes, Mama, and I'll be back to help you with the mending."

"Where're you two headed?"

"We're just going to explore along the creek, Mama."

"Well, don't be gone too long." Aubrey's mom gave her a hug. "Now, you two be careful and watch out for them bears," she said. "You know how I worry about you. You're all I have left in this world." Her good eye teared, and she dabbed at it with the corner of her apron. "Now scoot."

Chad hummed as he and Aubrey hurried off. By the time they reached the meadow, the sun shone brightly above the treetops. Bees buzzed as they went about their work. The drying grasses waved a welcome in the gentle breeze.

Chad searched the meadow for any signs of a bear. The wild raspberries were ripening—bears loved them.

"We are going to look for the cave, aren't we?" Aubrey brushed a wisp of red hair away from her face.

"Yup, but we have to watch for bears."

"Where should we start?"

"I think we should look by the edge of the meadow, where the boulders tumbled down the side of the mountain."

As Chad followed the trail with Aubrey close behind, he began to wonder if there really was an Ice Cave. Of course, Chad wanted it to be true but knew it might be just a story.

"One of our best hens disappeared," Aubrey said. "Ma

thinks a fox got it."

"Could have been. I saw one not too far from your place on the way over."

"Ma makes extra money selling them eggs in town." Aubrey patted her apron. "She's planning to save up some extra so she can buy me some shoes for winter."

"Don't like to think much about winter," Chad said. "Except this winter, I'll have a new baby brother or sister."

The expression on Aubrey's face turned sad. She stopped and took a deep breath.

"I'm sorry, Aubrey." Chad placed his hand on her shoulder. "I didn't mean to upset you."

"I know. It's just that this winter… I won't have Jesse."

Chad didn't know what to say, so they continued walking in silence. They followed the game trail across the meadow and into the trees that bordered the creek. The shade from the trees cooled them.

"We'd best stay far away from that," Chad said. "I'll have to let Pa know about it. It sure would be nice to have some sweet honey for cornbread."

That made Aubrey smile and lick her lips.

"Chad, I'm getting tired." Aubrey said, sitting down on a small boulder. "Maybe the old man was telling a story."

Chad sat next to Aubrey. "Maybe you're right." He wiped the sweat from his brow. Let's go just a little while longer. If we don't find it today, we'll go home. Okay?"

Aubrey shrugged her shoulders and stood up. "Okay."

Chad trudged along. He stopped and turned to Aubrey. "Wait! Did you feel that?"

"What?" Aubrey looked puzzled.

Chad started moving his hand in front of him, facing the mountainside.

"What? What do you see?" Aubrey swatted at a fly.

"Don't you feel it?" Chad asked excitedly. "It's coming from the boulders over there."

"What's coming?" Aubrey tossed her braids in frustration.

"Cold air. The cave must be nearby." Chad brushed some brown spruce needles off his shoulder and hurriedly started in the direction of the cold air.

"Wait for me!"

As Chad followed the cold draft, it grew stronger and stronger. He knew he must be close.

"We'd better be quiet. I don't want to startle anything." Chad took a deep breath. "Who knows what we might find."

Aubrey nodded her head in agreement.

When the air became really cold, Chad stopped. He peeked around some large granite boulders. He could feel the cold air but couldn't see where it was coming from. He searched in and out of the massive boulders. Chad looked closer—a dark opening in the boulders. The Ice Cave. He started toward the entrance when he heard noises inside the cave. Chad motioned Aubrey to get back behind the rocks.

A low growl came from the cave entrance. He heard shuffling sounds. The growl grew louder and deeper.

"Let's get out of here," Chad whispered, wide-eyed. "It could be a bear." He grabbed Aubrey's hand and pulled her away. Chad moved as fast as he could, and Aubrey followed close behind. He pushed aside the branches of thick leaves that blocked their way and scrambled farther and farther away until he tripped and fell hard on his knee.

"Are you alright?" Aubrey said, almost falling over him.

"I think so." He stood and rubbed his knee. "Let's go."

Chad fled until he felt safe again. He plopped down on a large rock by the creek.

Out of breath, he wiped the sweat from his upper lip. "I heard somethin' growling." He lifted his pant leg and found a large bruise on his knee.

"Do you think it was a bear?" Aubrey sat next to him. "Or was it a mountain lion?"

"No. It wasn't a bear. It sounded more like a dog or somethin'." Chad bit his lip.

"What was it then?"

"I don't know, but whatever it was, I think it heard or smelled us."

"Well, now we know there's a cave," Aubrey said, adjusting her apron.

"I guess the cave is trouble," Chad said, wincing as he rubbed his knee. "But now I'm more curious than ever to find out what's in there."

"Me, too, but I'm scared," Aubrey said. "Aren't you?"

"A little."

"A little? I'd say you were more than a little scared. You practically dragged me away."

Aubrey grinned. Chad blushed.

"I s'pose you're right." Chad stood up. "We'd better be more careful next time."

"Maybe we should bring some soldiers with us," Aubrey

teased.

"I don't think so. Besides, most of the soldiers from Fort McKinney are in the Dakotas helping with the Sioux uprising."

"Chad, what do you think we should do?"

"I think we should try again but come better prepared. I'll bring a lantern next time."

"We'd better get home. It's getting late, and Ma will be worried."

"You best not tell your Ma what we've been up to," Chad said.

"I won't tell her." Aubrey placed her hands on her hips. "I know better."

Chad shrugged. "I don't want nobody to know we've been lookin' for the cave. Who knows what might happen if they find out?"

ROUND CAT EYES

"Do bears like wild onions?" Aubrey asked Chad just as the widow pulled the buckboard wagon in front of the J.H. Conrad & Company General Store.

"I don't think so. Why?"

"Just wondering. Ma wanted me to find some for soup."

Chad hopped off the wagon and helped Mrs. Foster step down.

"You mind your manners in the store, and I'll treat you to a candy stick when I'm finished," Mrs. Foster said.

"I'll be good," Chad said with a grin.

Inside the store, Chad heard Mrs. Sawyer, Junior's mother, complaining loudly to the clerk. "I don't think it's civil to have a wild animal like that in town. Sheriff Mitchell should do something about it," she said sternly, then strutted out the door like a rooster in a huff.

"What was that all about?" Mrs. Foster asked.

"You don't need to be concerned, Mrs. Foster," the clerk said. "Mrs. Sawyer always gets her feathers all ruffled over something. What can I do for you?"

Mrs. Foster set her basket of eggs down on the counter. "I brought these eggs for sale, and I be needin' some cornmeal, a can of Calumet baking powder, salt, and some coffee."

While Mrs. Foster waited for her order, Aubrey examined the rainbow-colored display of ribbons, and Chad eyed the large glass jars of striped candy sticks and peppermint balls.

Two old men sat around a wooden barrel playing checkers in the center of the store. Chad walked over to the men and watched them.

"Porter, I reckon we need the wolfers to help protect the cattle," one of the men said as he crowned another king.

"I reckon, Splint, but the Indians hate 'em. Say their dogs get into the poison bait and kills 'em." He spat some tobacco juice into the spittoon.

"I know, but whatcha gonna do?" Splint scratched his fuzzy, gray beard.

Chad heard the door open and turned to see who had entered.

"Hello, Chad, Aubrey." The woman wearing a yellow sunbonnet tipped her head slightly.

"Oh, hi, Miss Bryant," Chad and Aubrey said together.

"I've missed seeing you since the statehood celebration. Are you enjoying the summer?" Miss Bryant asked, clutching her shawl.

"Yes, Miss Bryant," Aubrey said. "Chad and I have been exploring Clear Creek for the best places to pick chokecherries this fall. And we found—"

"We found a good fishin' hole," Chad interrupted. He scowled at Aubrey.

Miss Bryant looked at Chad curiously. "Well, that is wonderful. You two be careful now and enjoy yourselves. It won't be long before school starts again." Miss Bryant strolled to the other end of the store.

"Chad, why did you interrupt me?" she whispered. "I wasn't going to say anything about the cave." She placed her hands on her hips. "You don't trust me."

"Yah, I do, but I thought…" Chad stuffed his hands deep into his pockets.

"What?"

Outside the store, a lady screamed.

"What's goin' on?" Chad asked. He and Aubrey rushed toward the door.

A small crowd had gathered outside the store, watching a buckboard wagon loaded with supplies rattle down Main Street. Tied by a chain to the back of the wagon on one side, a scruffy-looking coyote panted. On the other side, a large gray wolf followed, tied with an even bigger chain. A grizzly-looking old feller, the driver, stopped momentarily to stare. He had a strange-looking face. Even from across the street, his big round eyes were visible. The man scowled at the crowd and spat on the ground. Then, he drove away, his wagon rumbling down the street in a cloud of dust.

"Come along, children," Mrs. Foster said from behind them, paying no attention to the crowd. "I need to get back."

"But, Mama, did you see that? He's got a—"

"No time for such nonsense. Let's board the wagon," she said.

Chad helped Mrs. Foster mount the wagon and settle in.

"Here's a peppermint stick for each of you."

"Thank you, Mama."

"Thanks, Mrs. Foster," Chad said. "This is my favorite. If I ever get rich, I'm gonna buy me a whole mess of candy sticks."

Mrs. Foster chuckled. "I'm sure you will."

The taste and smell of the peppermint stick made Chad very happy, but he wondered why anyone would bring a wolf or coyote into town.

"Chad," Aubrey said, "Who's the man with the big round eyes?"

"I don't know. I've seen him before but don't recall his name."

"Mama, do you know?"

"I heard people call him Wild something or other."

"Why do you suppose he's got a coyote and a wolf?" Aubrey asked.

"Don't know." Mrs. Foster turned to look at Aubrey. "Best you stay away from him. He don't appear to be none too friendly. You, too, Chad." She snapped the reins. "Besides, those two critters of his are wild and ain't nothin' to mess with."

After Chad left the Foster place, he met Junior and Brett walking along the road. Everybody called him Junior, but his real name was James Junior Sawyer. He and Brett were best friends. Brett was kind of quiet and shy. Junior was pushy like his mom, but he didn't bully Chad or Aubrey anymore since Chad had stood up to him at school last spring. Chad still didn't really like him, but Junior seemed friendlier now.

"Hey, Chad, whatcha been up to?"

"Not much since the statehood celebration." Chad smiled. "What about you?"

Junior kicked a rock in the road. "Caught some big fish the other day along the creek. Brett and me saw you and Aubrey out there a couple of times."

Brett nodded. He always agreed with whatever Junior said or told him to do.

"We were just out explorin', looking for chokecherry patches for pickin' come fall." Chad pushed his hands deep into his pockets and changed the subject. "You seen any bear signs lately?"

"Nope," Junior said. "But my dad has—over along the creek by the rockslide."

"You seen any?" Brett asked, fiddling with his bright red bandana neckerchief.

"Just some scat on the creek trail." Chad fidgeted.

"Wanna come fishin' with us sometime?" Brett asked. "Found us a mighty fine fishin' hole."

"Ah, he doesn't wanna go fishin' with us. I'll bet he and Aubrey's got a special spot already." Junior grinned at Chad. "Ain't that right?"

Chad shrugged and shook his head no. "Well, I best get home now. Ma's probably waitin' on me."

When Chad arrived home, Ma was sitting in her rocker on the front porch, snapping beans. She looked tired but gave him a gentle smile. "I felt the baby move."

Chad grinned. "I hope it's gonna be a boy."

"If it's a boy, I hope he's a lot like you."

"Ma, I saw an old man with big round eyes drivin' a buckboard in town today. He had a coyote and a wolf tied to the back of his wagon. Chad sat on the porch step next to her. "You ever seen him?"

"I have." She rested her hands in her lap for a moment. "The townfolk call him Wildcat Tom."

"What's he doin' with a wolf?" Chad beamed with curiosity.

"I don't rightly know, but it's dangerous to try and keep a wild thing. So don't you ever go near that man or his wolf," she said in a stern voice. "You hear me?"

"Yes, Ma. I won't," Chad said. Except…he was curious to know more about Wildcat Tom. What kind of man keeps a wolf?

BONES

On Sunday afternoon, the sky burned a bright summer blue. The Widow Foster and Aubrey ate dinner with Chad and his family. Chad's ma had baked a cinnamon cake that made the cabin smell heavenly. The widow brought a loaf of fresh sourdough bread and a jar of homemade chokecherry jelly. They had a fine meal, and while Chad ate his cake, Pa asked the widow if she had heard about a stagecoach robbery.

"Can't say that I have,"

"Sheriff Mitchell told me that it happened over by the south fork of the Powder River. The robber got away with gold and some jewelry."

Pa looked puzzled. "Can't imagine how one outlaw could get away with that. He must have been one sly fella."

Stunned at the sheriff's words, Chad glanced at Aubrey. What if the robber knew about the cave and had hidden the gold there? It was the perfect place to hide stolen goods.

"Pa, would it be alright if Aubrey and I went explorin' this afternoon?"

"It's fine with me if Mrs. Foster don't mind."

"I don't mind," Mrs. Foster said. "You might look for some wild onions."

"We will, Mama," Aubrey said.

Chad smiled. "Who knows what we'll find if we

look."

Grabbing a small cloth sack for wild onions, Chad and Aubrey took off to explore.

"Aubrey, wait. We'd better take a lantern with us this time. I'll grab one from the shed."

The August sun shone bright, and a hot, dry wind blew over the withering grasses. No bears were in sight in the meadow, and the deer must have been resting in the cool shade of the trees bordering the meadow.

"I was thinking," Chad said. "What if the robber hid the stolen gold in the Ice Cave?"

"Do you really think he did?"

"Sure. It would be a safe place. Who would look for it there?"

The thought of finding the gold made Chad excited. Maybe today would be the day he got rich.

"I feel like somebody's watching us," Chad said.

"Looks like somebody's over on the far side of the meadow." Aubrey pointed toward the edge where the trees bordered the browning grasses.

"I don't see anybody." Chad shrugged. "Probably somebody pickin' berries."

"Might be Junior and Brett. I thought I saw something bright red."

"No, don't s'pose so." Chad laughed. "It's too hot for Junior to be out doin' somethin'."

Aubrey giggled.

Chad wiped the sweat from his brow. "It sure is hot. Pa says we be needin' rain, or the whole ranch is gonna dry up and blow away."

"I don't mind none," Aubrey said. "I'd rather be hot than cold like I was most of last winter."

"It sure was a long winter." Chad looked thoughtful as he scratched his head.

"Whatcha thinkin' about?"

"I wonder why they call it the Ice Cave. You s'pose it has ice in it?"

Aubrey shrugged. "It's summer. I don't think so."

Chad switched the lantern to his other hand. "Pa warned me. I'd better be careful with the lantern. Wouldn't want to start a fire."

Tears came to Aubrey's eyes, and she sniffled.

"What's the matter?" Chad asked, but then he remembered. "Oh, I'm sorry, Aubrey. I forgot about what happened to your pa."

Aubrey wiped the tears away. "I know you didn't mean no harm."

Chad felt bad, so he changed the subject. "Let's cool off in the creek."

Aubrey gave a nod and smiled.

Chad started to hurry when he heard the creek singing. He rolled up his britches and stepped out into the clear water just up to his knees. "Whoa! That's cold."

Aubrey sheepishly joined him.

"Feels mighty good once you get used to it," Chad said. He gave Aubrey a mischievous look.

"Don't you—"

Chad started laughing and splashing Aubrey. She splashed back.

"You're onery, Chad," she said, her face and hair dripping.

"We'd better get going." He stepped out of the water. "That was fun, but I really want to find out what's in that cave."

Then, he remembered the growling he had heard the last time he was there. What was it?

They continued along the creek, following the game trail until they felt cold air. This time, they cautiously approached the cave. It appeared to be unoccupied.

"I don't see or hear anythin'," Chad said.

Standing in front of the cave, Chad let the cold air cool his face. He wondered how far into the mountain the cave extended. He lit the lantern and peered into the dark opening of the cave. It wasn't much higher than a tall cowboy and about as wide as a wagon wheel.

"I'm glad you remembered the lantern," Aubrey said. "It's awfully dark in there."

"Don't worry. I don't see any bear scat or paw prints. I don't think we'll find a bear inside." Chad took a deep breath. "Let's go."

The narrow entrance to the cave widened as it burrowed into the mountainside. Chad held the lantern carefully as he stepped into the darkness. His right hand touched the cool rocky wall—cold and damp. Aubrey followed him in silence. The lantern light cast an eerie shadow, sending a shiver of excitement through Chad.

"Look, Aubrey! Over there! Somebody's had a campfire in here." Chad pointed to a small circle of rocks on the cave floor. Ashes filled the ring. A log stump for a seat rested next to it. Chad noticed some large animal prints on the dirt floor.

His eyes were as wide as saucers. "Look! These are paw prints from a wolf."

"This proves that Wildcat Tom has been here," Aubrey said. "Do you think he's the outlaw who committed the robbery over by Powder River?"

"I don't know, but he could be." Chad's heart beat like a soldier's drum. "Let's see what's ahead."

The cave narrowed a bit more as they continued deeper into the darkness. Water droplets dripped off the ceiling. They followed the dark passageway until it opened into a large open space. There, the cave appeared to end.

He carefully searched the side walls. Chad held the lantern up higher and surveyed the space.

Aubrey stepped back and gasped. "A skull!"

Chad shone the light on the stark white skull. A jawbone with several teeth and some other bones surrounded it. "It's only a deer skull. Somebody must have had venison for supper."

"It's still creepy," Aubrey said.

"Aubrey, look at this. They're some old Indian drawings on the wall."

The light revealed what appeared to be people with spears hunting an elk.

"Who did this?" Aubrey asked as she ran her fingers over the pictures.

"My pa told me about this. They're called petroglyphs." Chad looked closer. "Ancient people scratched pictures on the rock. These are old."

"I can't wait to tell Ma," Aubrey said.

"No, you can't." Chad shook his head. "If you do, she'll

know we were probably in a cave."

"Wait. What's that over there?" Chad moved toward the back wall. "It looks like a smaller opening off to the right. The ceiling was lower, and there was a rock shelf. Maybe somethin's hidden in there." He raised the lantern to get a closer look. "Somethin's in the back. Looks like a small wooden chest. Let's get a closer look."

"What if it's the stolen gold?" Aubrey clasped her hands together.

As Chad stepped back into the darkness of the chamber, he heard a fluttering above his head. His heart pounded like a fence post being hammered into the ground. He could feel Aubrey trembling next to his shoulder. The cold darkness smelled musty. He wished he were outside in the warm safety of the sun. Nervous sweat beaded on his forehead.

Chad tried to stand and see in the faint lantern light. The side of his face brushed against something soft and warm. He jerked and banged his head on the rock ceiling.

"Ouch!"

Suddenly, a flurry of movement circled his head. Whatever was in the chamber didn't matter now.

"Run, Aubrey! Run!!"

With lowered head, Chad ran toward the entrance of the cave, still carrying the lantern. Aubrey followed right behind him. Chad stumbled over the fire pit. He saw a cloud of black wings in the dim lantern light. Aubrey stopped and helped him up. Luckily, the lantern didn't break. Chad raced into the bright light, squinting to see what danger awaited him. He glanced around the front of the cave.

"I don't see anybody. Do you?"

"No." Aubrey shook her head. "What happened? You're bleeding."

"Bats! I stuck my head into some bats, and I banged my head on the rock wall." Chad looked pale as white thimble berries except for a trickle of blood on his forehead. "I hate bats."

"They scare me, too." Aubrey frowned. "I wonder what was in the chest?"

"I don't know, but I don't want to go back into the cave while the bats are in a frenzy. Let's go. We'll have to come back another time."

A SMALL WOODEN CHEST

Several days passed before Chad and Aubrey had a chance to go back to the cave. It still hadn't rained, so everything was bone dry. The creek was lower now, and in many places, it was low enough to walk across. The game trail was dusty, and the grasses crunched beneath their feet. The chokeberry bushes were laden with clusters of wine-colored berries. Even the air had a warm smell to it. Hoppers jumped like popcorn in the grasses, eating the dried stalks, and buzzing flies became more annoying.

Chad flicked a hopper off his shoulder. "Do you remember how bad the hoppers were last year?"

"How could I forget?" Her eyes opened wide. "They ate up a lot of Mama's garden."

"Pa told me when he was growing up in Nebraska that the hoppers appeared in swarms like dark clouds in the sky. Millions of them landed and ate everything in sight—corn and wheat crops and even a leather harness."

"I don't think the hoppers will be that bad this year."

"Pa said he read in the *Buffalo Echo* that we need to be prepared for wildfires. There was a big prairie fire down by Kaycee. He's plannin' to clear the grasses from around the house and barn. Said we was gonna help your Ma do the same thing."

"Your pa's a fine man."

Yes, Pa was a fine man, but what would Pa think about him stealing somebody's wooden chest?

As Chad and Aubrey continued to walk, hoppers continued to pop around them. They swatted at the flies and hoppers while the summer sun beat down on them.

Chad wondered what could be in the small wooden chest. He wondered even more why Tom had a pet wolf. What should he do if he found the wolf guarding the cave entrance when they got there?

When Chad and Aubrey arrived at the cave, they checked to make sure nobody had followed them. No wolf was guarding the entrance. Upon entering the cave, Chad cautiously searched the ceiling for bats. He figured the bats would leave him alone if he didn't brush up against them.

At the back of the cave, the lantern light shown on the place where the smaller opening was tucked away. Carefully holding the lantern, Chad let it shine in the farthest corner of the space. Aubrey stayed close to him.

Chad gasped. "Look, Aubrey! It's a small wooden chest."

"Do you suppose there's gold in it?"

"I don't know, but it has a lock on it." Chad thought for a moment. "Maybe there's a key hidden along the wall somewhere."

Out of nowhere, a light suddenly shown on them. Chad whirled around.

"What you doin' in here?" a raspy voice shouted.

In their excitement, they hadn't heard somebody approaching them from behind.

In the dim lantern light, a grizzly face with large round eyes appeared. Chad and Aubrey froze. Wildcat Tom.

"Uh…uh…we was just explorin'." Chad managed to say.

"Git! You ought not to be here. Now scoot before I—"

"We was just leavin'. Honest." As Chad passed close by him, he smelled his tobacco breath and felt the anger in the man's voice.

"And don't come back or tell anyone what you just seen."

They rushed to the cave entrance and stumbled into the blinding light. A deep growl greeted them. They stopped dead in their tracks. Chained to a nearby tree, a scruffy-looking wolf sneered at them. For a moment, Chad stood mesmerized by the wild creature before him. Then, it snapped at them with its sharp white fangs. Startled, Chad urged Aubrey to hightail it down the path before the animal tried to tear them apart.

Chad and Aubrey ran for their lives. Once they were far enough from the cave to feel safe, Chad, gasping for air, stopped short. Aubrey nearly climbed up his back.

"That was a close call." Chad tried to catch his breath. "Tom's hidin' somethin' in that cave. Somethin' mighty important."

"What do you think it is?" Aubrey asked.

Chad thought for a moment. "Maybe it's gold. Maybe he's the robber."

"Should we tell Sheriff Mitchell?"

"No," Chad said. He paused. "We have to find out what's in the chest first."

"How can we do that?" Aubrey pushed back sweaty strands of fiery-red wisps of hair from her face.

"We'll have to go back, and the next time make sure Tom's

not anywhere around.

As Chad and Aubrey headed home, they met Junior and Brett carrying their fishing poles. Junior held up three fish for them to see.

"What do you think? S'pose they'll be good eatin'?"

"Sure look so," Chad said.

"What you and her been doin' out there?"

Aubrey spoke quickly. "We've just been cooling off. Right, Chad?"

Chad swallowed hard and nodded in agreement.

"Why you got a lantern with ya?" Junior asked.

"Uh...we..." Chad started to say.

"We best be going, Chad. My ma will be wondering about us."

"She's not the only one who's wonderin'." Junior nudged Brett with his elbow, and they both snickered.

When Chad returned home, Pa asked him if he saw anything interesting while he was out exploring. "Did you see any bear?" Pa asked.

"No, but we did poke our toes in the creek to cool off."

"Can't blame ya. It was mighty hot today." Pa looked Chad in the eye. "I want you to be real careful. Everythin's tinder dry. If a fire started...well, it would be mighty bad."

"I know, Pa. I will be."

"Be on the lookout for a mama bear and her two cubs. I've seen 'em out on the meadow by the creek." Pa grinned. "You don't want to mess with no mama bear."

"Pa, could Aubrey and me go pickin' chokecherries tomorrow?"

Pa smiled. "I reckon if you get the stalls cleaned out, finish choppin' some firewood, and haul some more water for your ma, it'd be fine."

"Thanks, Pa." Chad headed for the wood pile.

"Your ma would sure appreciate some chokecherries, so she can make us some jelly and syrup for our griddle cakes." Pa winked.

"Yes, sir."

Chad thought this would be a good excuse to return to the cave. He could hardly wait to find out what was in the small wooden chest. If it was gold, what would he do? Would it be right to steal it if it was already stolen? He'd have to ask Pastor Duell on Sunday.

FURY

In the distance, Chad and Aubrey saw the symmetrical peak called North Ridge and Fort McKinney, built not far from its base. Clear Creek flowed out of the mountains near the fort and was about a two- or three-mile walk from Chad's cabin. Chad wanted to get close to the fort so he could listen to the Regimental Band play and watch the soldiers do their routine inspections. He often wished he could be a soldier and wear the blue uniform with gold buttons.

Soon, they clearly saw the huge flagpole of the fort. It looked like a mast of a sailing ship he'd seen in a picture. His pa had told him that a man named William Daley made it. He had lived in New England and made masts for sailing ships.

As they neared the fort, trumpets and drums blared from the parade grounds. Fort McKinney had been built in 1877 to help protect and keep order along the Bozeman Trail. It was home to the 10th African American Cavalry, otherwise known as the Buffalo Soldiers. Chad enjoyed listening to the military band practice on the parade grounds whenever possible.

"I might like to play the trumpet someday," Chad said. "Or a drum." He tapped a beat on his thigh.

Aubrey smiled with a twinkle in her eye. "I like how shiny the trumpets are."

They watched the band for a while until Chad said, "We'd better get along if we want to find out what's in the wooden chest."

"You're right. I hope it's gold," Aubrey said, clutching her folded hands to her heart.

Chad and Aubrey hurried along their way. The sun, still high in the sky, continued drying out everything in the meadow; the grasses softly rattled in the breeze. Chad was glad he had his new hat. He watched for bears that might be feasting on wild raspberries.

Chad came to an abrupt stop. "Don't move, Aubrey," he whispered. "Look over there." He pointed toward a clump of bushes.

Aubrey made an audible gasp. "A mother bear and her cubs!"

Chad gestured for Aubrey to back away. Fortunately, the bear was upwind and hadn't seen them.

"We'd better stay on the far side of the meadow," Chad said. "Pa warned me about her."

When they reached the far side of the meadow, Chad followed the creek trail again. He proceeded cautiously as he neared the Ice Cave. Chad saw the figure of a man and what looked like a dog in front of the cave. He stopped and waited to get a closer look.

The man checked to see if anyone was coming and disappeared into the cave entrance. Chad froze. He recognized that bearded face. Wildcat Tom. And that was no dog—it was his wolf.

"What's wrong?"

"Aubrey, it's Wildcat Tom, and he's got his wolf with him."

"Do you think he's counting his gold?"

"I don't know. I'm thinkin' he's an outlaw." Chad turned and looked Aubrey right in the eyes. "There must be gold."

"What do you think we should do?"

"Let's wait here and see if he comes out. Then, we can sneak back into the cave."

"If it is gold, we could be rich." Aubrey quietly clapped her hands.

Chad frowned. "We can't take stolen gold. It's not right." Chad thought for a moment. "But if it's stolen, there might be a reward."

Chad and Aubrey looked at each other, wondering what to do. They waited a long time for Wildcat Tom to come out of the cave, but he never did.

"I feel like somebody's watching us," Chad said.

"You don't see anybody, do you?"

"No, it's just a feelin'." Chad shuffled around nervously. "Probably nothin' to worry about."

"We've been gone a while. Mama worries something fierce." Aubrey fidgeted. "I don't want to trouble her."

"You're right, but we need to pick chokecherries before we head back, or Pa will be wonderin' what we were up to. We should probably leave and come back another time. It wouldn't be good if Tom ran into us on the trail."

They returned to the meadow far away from the creek trail, found several chokecherry bushes, and filled the old lard pail with berries. The scent of the fresh chokecherries made Chad crave chokecherry syrup.

"I saw that, Chad," Aubrey said with a stern look. "You'd

better not eat too many, or there won't be any jelly or syrup for either of us."

"I couldn't help it," he said, licking his berry-stained fingers.

Chad and Aubrey continued to pick the small berry clusters since it took a lot of chokecherries to make anything. They failed to notice a huge dark cloud on the mountain top behind them. A blinding flash of lightning and an ear-piercing crack of thunder split the silence. It slid directly toward them, over the mountain like syrup on a biscuit. The wind suddenly picked up and turned cold. Chad looked up—a curtain of white hail stretched across the dark-gray sky.

"Aubrey, hurry! I'll grab the pail. You carry the lantern. That hail is coming right at us!"

Chad and Aubrey scurried down the trail toward a large grove of cottonwoods, but the hail caught up with them. Soon, large balls of hail hurtled at them through the trees, scratching and bruising them. Cold shards of ice pounded their heads while leaves and branches battered them from all angles. Chad searched for more shelter to protect them.

Another flash of lightning lit up the sky. Seconds later, a frightening crack of thunder shook the ground. Chad pulled Aubrey behind a huge fallen tree trunk wedged between some large boulders. It provided some relief from the onslaught of hail. They covered their heads to protect them from the hail and falling debris.

The storm's fury lasted only a few minutes, but it seemed much longer than that. When the deluge was over, Chad and Aubrey crawled out from beneath the tree trunk. A light rain continued to fall, but the wind and hail stopped.

"Are you okay, Aubrey?" Chad brushed off wet cottonwood leaves from his arms and head.

"I'm okay, but I was scared."

"We'd better get home. Our folks are probably worried sick because of the storm."

When Chad returned home, his mother saw him coming and rushed out to meet him.

"Are you alright?" She looked at the scratches on his face and hands.

He handed her the pail of chokecherries. "Aubrey and I were pickin' chokecherries. We didn't see the storm comin'. Sorry, Mom."

"Let's get you cleaned up." She sighed. "You need to watch the sky more closely."

"Ma, what would you do if I found gold?"

His mother paused and looked around the cabin and thought for a moment. "I guess I'd buy me some new baby clothes and fill up the pantry with more supplies for the winter."

"Why do you ask?"

He smiled, "Just wonderin'."

"What would you do?"

Chad thought for a second. "I guess I'd buy you that pretty blue dress you saw at the mercantile and a new rifle for Pa."

"That's sweet, Chad, but what about you? Surely, there's something you'd like for yourself."

"I guess I'd like some new britches. Mine are kind of small."

"Well, you are growin', and so are your feet!"

Ma looked at Chad. "You plannin' on diggin' for gold?"

Chad shrugged. "Just dreamin', I guess."

"Dreamin' s not a bad thing." Ma clutched her hands around her middle and smiled. "Right now, I need you to fetch me a pail of water."

Chad headed outside to the well by the wood pile. Turning, he saw a large bull snake curled next to him. Bull snakes ate mice and helped keep their numbers down. He knew it wasn't poisonous, but it could still bite. So, he cautiously stepped back from the snake, picked up a chunk of pine, and tossed it at the snake. The snake uncoiled and slithered away.

As he pulled the bucket up from the well, his thoughts wandered back to the cave. What was in that small wooden chest? Could it be a chest of gold? Who did it belong to? If it was stolen gold, would it be right to keep it? All these questions tumbled around in his head like a tumbleweed on a blustery day. Would finding the answer to his question change everything?

BARED TEETH

The Skinner Freight Wagons arrived from Casper early in the day. Twenty-five multiple covered wagons were connected and pulled by seven- to nine-yoked pairs of oxen or mules. The caravan included a kitchen wagon, a wagon master, and a crew of about thirty-five men, leaving little room to maneuver on Main Street.

It was a sight to behold. Folks from far and wide filled the dusty street. The town was a flurry of activity. Men busied themselves unloading supplies at J.H. Conrad & Company's big log store and Foot's Store. Sun-bonneted ladies chatted on the wooden sidewalks; suspendered men talked about the hot, dry weather. Horses snorted and whinnied in the hot sun.

Chad's folks brought their wagon into town to gather supplies. The widow and Aubrey followed close behind. Chad and Aubrey met each other at Conrad's store. Chad hoped Ma would buy him some peppermint balls or striped candy sticks while Pa checked out a new Winchester rifle.

"If we get a reward, we can buy all the candy we want, Aubrey."

"What reward?" a familiar voice interrupted from behind him.

"Junior! I didn't see you." Chad tugged at the straps of his bib overalls.

"You shouldn't sneak up on people," Aubrey said.

"What reward?" Junior repeated.

Chad glanced at Aubrey and swallowed hard. "Oh, I...I... Pa said he'd reward me if I found a lost calf."

Junior squinted at Chad. "I think you're making that up."

"No, he's not," Aubrey added. "Honest."

"Chad, could you come over here?" Pa called out. "I want you to see this."

"Be right there, Pa." Chad turned with a jerk. "Gotta go, Junior."

It made Chad nervous to think that Junior had overheard him. Hopefully, he would forget about it.

Later, Pa told Chad to check out the freighters while he took care of some business at First National Bank. He warned Chad to be careful around the freighters. Aubrey joined him. Chad and Aubrey hadn't seen this many people since the Celebration of Wyoming's statehood in July. It was almost as festive. Even Mayor Burritt was out and about.

Chad and Aubrey decided to walk to the end of the street by the courthouse. There, they could stand on the bridge and look for fish in Clear Creek since the water was running low like it usually did at the end of the summer—unless a thunderstorm dropped a ton of rain in the nearby mountains.

In all the hustle and bustle, Chad noticed everyone skittering out of the way of a buckboard wagon tied to a hitching rail. A coyote and a wolf were chained to the back of it.

"Aubrey, look!" He pointed toward the wagon. "It must be Wildcat Tom's," Chad said excitedly. "Let's get a closer look."

Chad and Aubrey crossed the street. They approached the wagon cautiously. The coyote paced nervously, but the large wolf sat like a stone-gray statue and stared at them. Chad felt like the wolf's eyes could see right through him. It sent a shiver down his spine.

"Don't get too close," Aubrey reminded him.

The wolf moved toward Chad, snarled, and bared its teeth. Chad jumped back, and the wolf lashed out at him, just missing his arm.

"Git away!"

Startled, Chad looked up to see Wildcat Tom carrying a big burlap sack over his shoulder. He was headed toward the wagon.

"You leave Granite alone. He could tear you apart." Wildcat Tom heaved the sack onto the back of the wagon." He spat and wiped his mouth with the back of his hand.

Up close, Chad saw how big Tom's eyes were and how his bushy eyebrows collided on his wrinkled forehead. His facial expression resembled that of a wildcat. Chad wondered if he was as dangerous.

"We was just wantin' to see it up close," Chad said in a trembling voice. "We didn't mean no harm."

Wildcat Tom stared at them with his big round eyes opened really wide. "Ain't you the young'uns I seen in the cave?"

Chad and Aubrey backed away, too afraid to answer.

"Git!" Tom raised a fist at Chad. "Don't need any young'uns botherin' what's mine."

Chad and Aubrey hightailed it back to their folks.

"What's wrong, Chad?" Pa asked. "You look as white as a snow-covered mountain peak."

Aubrey pointed toward the end of the street, but she couldn't see Tom's wagon heading out of town. "It was Wildcat Tom's wolf! It nearly got Chad."

"What were you doin' hangin' round that beast?" Pa asked.

"We just wanted to get a better look at it," Chad said.

"You best stay as far away as you can from old Tom's critters." Pa placed his hand on Chad's shoulder. "I mean it."

"Yes, Pa. Do you know anythin' about him?"

"Well," Pa adjusted his hat. "He's a trapper and a prospector from Nebraska. A wolfer, too. Poisons wolves that raid the horse herds at Fort Reno. Like I says, you best stay away from him."

Chad nodded. "But why does he keep a wolf?"

"Can't say that I know." Pa brushed his rust-colored mustache with his finger. "I do know that the Indians hate him cuz many of their dogs eat the poisoned bait he sets out."

On the way home, Chad couldn't help but think that Wildcat Tom could be an outlaw, too. He probably had gold in the box hidden in the cave. Chad needed to find out.

The next day, Chad finished his chores early. He weeded the vegetable garden, brought in firewood, and hauled water in the wooden buckets for Ma. After his chores were completed, he offered to search for wild onions with Aubrey if her mom would allow it. So, he grabbed a lantern when Ma wasn't looking and hustled over to the Foster place to pick up Aubrey.

"Aubrey, I'm thinkin' Tom must be an outlaw," Chad said as they left the Foster place. "He seems mighty mean."

"His wolf's not very friendly, either." Aubrey shivered.

While crossing the meadow by the creek, they saw the sow, the mother black bear, and her two cubs again. She lumbered out from a clump of cottonwoods. Chad and Aubrey were downwind, so they quietly walked away and hugged the edge of the other side of the meadow.

Then, without warning, a boar, a large male black bear, appeared in the distance where they were headed. Chad wasn't sure what to do. If he kept moving forward, he would meet up with the male. If he turned back, he might run into the mother and her cubs. Chad froze. Aubrey grabbed his arm.

"What should we do?" she whispered.

"I'm not sure."

Chad decided it might be better to turn around and hope the mother didn't wander any closer to them. He motioned Aubrey to follow him, keeping his eyes on the mother bear, whose sleek black coat glistened in the sunlight. She seemed to be moving more toward them. The wind suddenly changed direction as it often did in the late afternoon. The mother bear stood on her hind legs and sniffed the air. Had she caught a whiff of them?

The sow woofed and sent the cubs back into the trees. She started to charge toward Chad and Aubrey but then stopped. Was she bluffing? She stood again, but this time when she sniffed the air, she looked away from them and in the direction of the boar. Then, from the other side of the meadow, charged the lumbering bear. In moments, the two bears collided.

Chad knew that a mother bear would defend her cubs to the death. It was horrible to watch them tear into each other. Loud, angry growls shattered the peace of the meadow as the bears lashed out at each other. The two bears rose on their hind legs and slashed at each other with powerful dagger-sharp claws.

Growling and snorting, they savagely attacked each other. Chad heard their jaw-clacking teeth. Then, the mother bear's long, sharp claws sliced a large gash in one of the boar's ears, causing him to throw his massive head back and fall onto all fours. Her furor sent the giant off in the opposite direction from her cubs.

Stunned, Chad grabbed Aubrey's arm and pulled her away from the bears.

"We'd better turn around and get home before she remembers we're here."

Chad and Aubrey decided to take the road back—to be safe. That's when they saw Junior and Brett, both out of breath, running up to them.

"I know you saw that mama bear fightin'," Junior said. "About scared me out of my britches."

"Me, too," Brett said.

"It was awful." Aubrey tightened her bonnet.

"What were you doin' out in the meadow?" Junior asked.

"We was lookin' for wild onions," Chad sheepishly replied.

Junior gave Chad a puzzled expression. "Do you always use a lantern when you pick wild onions?"

Chad and Aubrey looked at each other.

"I know you're up to somethin'." Junior crossed his arms. "Maybe lookin' for somethin' stolen?"

"None of your business, Junior." Aubrey stomped her foot.

"Well, I'll find out." Junior backed off. "You'll see."

When Chad and Aubrey arrived at the Foster place, they decided not to tell anyone about the bear fight. If Mrs. Foster or Ma and Pa found out, they might not be able to go to the meadow for a long time. Now, they had to worry about Junior finding out about the cave. Junior was sneaky. They would have to keep a close eye on him as well as the bears.

FORTUNE

"Chad, I need you to go into town and pick up some sugar so I can finish making my berry preserves." Ma wiped her hands on her calico-print apron. She reached into her pocket and pulled out a few coins. She handed him the money. "Be careful not to lose this," she said sternly. "It's all I have left until we sell some more eggs."

"Yes, Ma. I'll be real careful." He placed the coins deep in his trouser pocket.

"You might stop by and see if Mrs. Foster needs anything in town."

"Yes, Ma." Chad grabbed his worn straw hat and left.

When Chad reached the Foster place, he found Aubrey feeding the chickens. Mrs. Foster was churning butter.

"Good day, Mrs. Foster. You need anythin' in town? I'm gonna pick up some sugar for my ma."

The widow wiped her forehead with the back of her hand. She smiled. "Not today, but thanks for asking."

"Ma, can I go with Chad?" Aubrey clasped her hands and gave her ma a pleading look.

"If you're done with your chores."

"Yes, Ma. I'm done."

"Alright, then, but be back in time for supper."

Chad and Aubrey hurried off. The sky was clear, the air still, and the road dry and dusty. Several deer crossed the road in front of them. Then, off in the distance, a wagon headed their way.

"I wonder who that could be?" Aubrey asked, brushing a fly off her arm.

"It's hard to tell, but there's somethin' different about that wagon." Chad squinted to try and see it better. "Do you hear somebody singin'?"

"I think so." Aubrey cupped her hand by her ear. "Yes, somebody is singing."

"I hear bells jingling, too," Chad said.

As the wagon drew nearer, the singing grew louder. This was no regular wagon. It was painted a bright red and decorated with an ornate gold trim. A sign on the wagon read **Matthew Martin Medicine Man** in bold red letters. A distinguished-looking man and a beautiful lady sat in the seat. A pair of prancing black horses with bells on their harnesses pulled up next to Chad and Aubrey. The driver of the wagon stopped singing and stepped down from the wagon. The man, dressed in a black vest, white silk scarf, and red coattails, wore a shiny black top hat. He tipped his hat and gave a hearty "Hello. I'm Matthew Medicine Man." He smiled broadly and pointed to the woman wearing a frilly white blouse and cherry red skirt. She remained seated in the wagon. "This is Jenny Jasmine, fortune teller supreme." The woman waved and nodded. The gentleman proceeded to dust off his vest. "And who do I have the pleasure of meeting?" He looked with interest at Chad.

"I'm Chad Ryan, and this is my friend Aubrey." Chad pushed his hands deep into his pockets.

"Wonderful that our paths should cross," Matthew said.

"This is your lucky day!"

"It is?" Chad gawked. Aubrey smiled hopefully.

Matthew placed his hand on Chad's shoulder. "I have something amazing to show you." He opened two doors on the side of his wagon, revealing shelves of bottles of various sizes. He stretched out his arms toward the display.

"You see with your own eyes miracle medicines. There is no sore my elixirs will not heal, no pain they will not subdue. I have blood and liver pills." He stood proudly. "My elixirs were prepared in my laboratory in Chicago. Guaranteed to work."

Chad thought about his pa's bad back. "Can it heal back pain?"

Matthew reached for a green bottle and held it out to Chad. "This, my boy, will take away his pain."

Chad reached for the bottle and held it carefully. "Will it really?"

"Trust me, young man. Your pa will be proud of you and grateful."

"How much does it cost?" Chad took the coins out of his pocket.

Matthew scratched his chin thoughtfully for a moment. "You seem like a decent, caring son. You can have it for just 15 cents."

Ma had given Chad 25 cents. He would still have 10 cents left if he bought it. Would that be enough to buy sugar? Surely, she would want him to buy medicine that would help his pa. What should he do?

Chad sighed and handed Matthew 15 cents. "I'll take it."

The beautiful woman stepped down from the wagon and

walked over to Chad.

"You seem worried about buying the elixir," she said sympathetically. "But I feel something good is about to happen to you. Would you like me to tell your fortune?"

Before Chad could answer, Aubrey interrupted. "Are you a fortune teller?"

"Yes, my sweet girl." Jenny placed her hand over her heart. "It is my gift."

"A real fortune teller?" Chad asked. Jenny nodded. "Then, I want you to tell me my fortune."

"I will get ready," Jenny said.

Chad looked at Aubrey. "I can hardly wait!"

After a few minutes, Jenny called Chad and Aubrey over to a table she had set up by the back of the wagon. She invited them to be seated. A large crystal globe sat in front of Jenny. She placed a sheer white veil over her head and proceeded to speak while circling her hands over the globe.

"Oh, mystery of mysteries, speak to me." She closed her eyes. "Tell me, tell me true. Tell me what I ask of you." Her hands began circling faster and faster. "What is the future of this boy Chad?" She gasped.

"What is it? What's happening?" Chad asked.

"Hush, the spirits are speaking. I cannot hear them."

Chad grabbed Aubrey's hand and squeezed it. Sweat bubbled on his forehead; his breathing grew shallow.

Jenny puffed up as if filled with some kind of spirit. She stared into the crystal ball and mumbled something. Then, her hands trembled, her mouth opened wide, and she uttered a cry. "The spirits say you will meet a man, a special man."

"Is it an old man with a scruffy beard?" Chad interrupted.

"Wait, he is a strange man. He travels alone and has a secret."

"Does he have a wolf?"

Jenny held her right hand up. "Silence! This man will make you rich."

Chad turned to Aubrey. "Did you hear that?" he whispered. "It must be Wildcat Tom."

"When will he meet this man?" Aubry asked.

Jenny gazed deeper into the crystal ball. "The spirits say it will be soon. But wait! They say you must be very careful and…" Suddenly, she collapsed.

"What's wrong? What's happening?" Chad said, alarmed.

Jenny raised her head. She put her hand to her forehead in a very dramatic movement. "It's over…the spirits are gone."

Chad and Aubrey stood up. The future prediction left Chad dizzy. Wildcat Tom was going to make Aubrey and him rich.

"Are you alright?" Chad asked Jenny.

"I will be fine. It's exhausting entering the spirit world."

"We'd better go," Chad said.

"Wait. You need to pay me for your fortune." She removed her veil.

Chad looked puzzled. "You didn't say it would cost anythin'."

"It's very tiring work entering the spirit world."

Chad reached into his pocket for the ten cents he had left. "How much?"

She looked at the coins in his hand. "It is 10 cents. A small price to pay to know the future." Jenny shook her head. Her large gold hoop earrings caught the sun.

Chad hesitated. If he paid her the ten cents, he would not

have any money to buy sugar for Ma. Maybe it would not matter once he told her he was going to be rich. Surely, she would understand, or would she?

Chad thanked and paid Jenny the 10 cents he owed her. Matthew Martin, the Medicine Man, and Jenny, the fortune teller, quickly packed up the wagon. Then, singing and laughing, they turned the wagon around and headed south—away from Buffalo.

When Chad returned home, Ma greeted him at the door with her hands on her hips. "Where is the sugar? You didn't lose the money, did you?"

"No, Ma!" Chad spouted. He could hardly stay still. "The most wonderful thing happened to me." He handed Ma the green bottle. "I met this doctor, who sold me an elixir to cure Pa's back pain."

"What doctor? Where?"

Aubrey and I saw this special red wagon coming down the road. "We heard singing and the jingle of bells…and it stopped right by us. There was a sign on the wagon: **Mathew Martin Medicine Man**." Chad took a deep breath. "He had all kinds of medicine…cures for everything and—"

Ma put up her hands. "Stop! Oh, Chad! Did you spend all the money on the elixir?"

Chad looked confused. "No, but I thought the medicine would help Pa."

Ma scowled, "What did you do with rest of the money?"

"I had to pay Jenny?"

"Who is Jenny? Why?"

"Jenny was a fortune teller. She told me I was going to meet a man who would make me rich."

Ma wrang her hands. "Oh, Chad. You've been fooled. Fortune tellers cannot tell you the future. They trick you and lie and then take your money."

Chad's shoulders slumped. "Jenny was making it up?"

"I'm afraid so."

"What about the elixir?"

"Medicine men travel around the country selling their elixirs and pills. They talk big, but the medicines are usually just bottles of alcohol diluted with colored water."

"I'm not gonna get rich?" Tears filled Chad's eyes.

Ma placed her arm around his shoulders. "Not unless you work hard."

Chad could not believe he had been so foolish. He thought the elixir would help his pa. When he did get rich, he could help Ma and Pa. A part of him still believed that Wildcat Tom's treasure chest might make him rich.

DISAPPOINTMENT

"Are you sure nobody saw us?" Aubrey said as they approached the cave entrance.

"I don't think so, but let's hurry. I wouldn't want to get caught. If Tom finds us in here again, who knows what he might do."

Chad and Aubrey scurried to the back of the cave. It was a small wooden chest with a lock on it. Chad ran his hand over the top of it. They both stared at the chest. He gently lifted it and turned to Aubrey.

"It's not very heavy, but it could have gold in it." Chad rubbed his hand over the top of the box. "I wonder."

Chad heard a bit of a flutter on the cave ceiling. The bats were stirring. He waited a moment until they stopped.

"I wanna buy Ma somethin' for the new baby and a rifle for Pa." He looked at Aubrey. "What will you get for your ma?"

"Ma'd like a new dress, and I'd like a new apron."

"I'd like to buy a whole jar of peppermint sticks, too."

"So how are we going to open it?" Aubrey placed her hands on her hips.

Chad set the chest down. He raised the lantern and searched the cave wall. "Maybe the key is hidden close by."

Chad and Aubrey were so focused on finding a key that

they did not hear Tom creep up behind them.

"What do you think you're doin'? Why, I have a mind to whip both of you." Tom said through clenched teeth. "Git away from that chest. Now!"

Startled, Chad jumped back.

"You stole what's in that chest. Didn't you?" Chad asked. "You're an outlaw."

Tom spat on the cold ground. "I ain't no outlaw. What's in that box is mine, and you ain't got no right pokin' around what's not yours, anyway." Tom raised his fist at them. "Now git, or you'll regret the day you was born."

Chad and Aubrey quickly turned around and raced out of the cave. At the entrance, the wolf chained to a nearby tree bared his teeth, snarled, and lurched out at them. Aubrey screamed.

"Let's get out of here!" Chad shouted.

While tree branches clawed at them, Chad and Aubrey stumbled away from the cave, tripping over rocks and logs. Out of breath, they both stopped to rest when they felt safe. Something caught his eye when he looked back toward the cave.

"What is it, Chad?"

"Thought I saw somebody hidin' in the trees."

Aubrey stared off into the distance. "I don't see anything."

"I don't see nobody now, but I know I saw somethin'."

Aubrey fidgeted with her hands. "Who do you think it was? Or what?" Images of the bear attack crossed her mind.

Chad shrugged. "I don't know for sure, but we'd better get goin'."

The wind picked up and rattled the dry grasses as Chad and Aubrey hustled back home.

"Guess we were wrong."

"I know." Chad sighed. "No gifts for the baby or rifle for Pa."

"No new dress for Ma, no new apron for me." Aubrey hung her head; her dreams had vanished.

Chad glanced at Aubrey. "And no candy, either," he said.

Aubrey's lips pouted.

"What if we're wrong?" Chad stopped and pulled on the strap of his bib overalls. "Tom could be lyin', ya know."

"I guess." Aubrey straightened her bonnet.

"What else could be so important that he would hide a small chest in a cave?"

Aubrey shrugged. "Don't know. Does seem suspicious."

In the distance, two soldiers galloped toward them.

"Wonder what they're after?" Chad scratched his head.

"Maybe they're looking for the outlaws."

As they drew closer, the soldiers slowed their horses and stopped beside them. The horses shook their heads and snorted.

"Howdy," one of the soldiers said. "Where you headed?"

"We was just out walkin'," Chad said. Nervously, he swung the lantern at his side.

One of the soldiers looked Chad in the eyes. "You seen anybody out here?" The soldier tightened his reins.

Chad looked over at Aubrey and back to the soldier. "No, sir. Nobody else out here in the meadow." He swallowed hard.

"You sure?" The soldier stared at Chad. He felt like the soldier could see right into his head. "We're looking for an outlaw. Stole some gold."

"Yes, sir." Chad wiped the sweat from his brow with the back of his hand. His eyes shifted toward Aubrey. She glanced down at the ground.

"Well, you two, be careful. This man is dangerous. No tellin' what he might do if you come upon him." The soldier tipped his cap and resumed his trek toward town.

After the soldiers left, Aubrey turned to Chad. "Maybe Tom is the outlaw, but you lied, Chad." She grimaced.

"No, Aubrey. We didn't see anybody out here in the meadow. Tom was in the cave."

Several days later when Chad was eating supper, he heard a wagon pull up outside the cabin.

"Who could that be?" Ma asked.

"I'll find out," Pa said, getting up from the table.

He opened the door and stepped outside. Ma and Chad followed.

Wildcat Tom stepped down out of his rickety wagon. The chained wolf stared with cold eyes and bared teeth from behind it. The coyote paced next to the wolf.

"Whatcha mean bringing them wild critters here on my land?" Pa asked.

Tom squinted his eyes and moved closer toward Chad, so close he could smell the foul breath of the old man. He pointed a shaky finger at Chad, who was standing to the left side of Ma. "I reckon he knows." He spat and wiped brown drool from the side of his mouth with the back of his hand.

Pa turned toward Chad. "What's he talking about, Chad?"

"I…I…I don't know, Pa." Chad squirmed and plunged his

hands deep into his pockets. His stomach tightened with the lie. He could hardly breathe.

"He ain't telling the truth!" Tom said and spat again. "My wooden chest is gone!"

"Now, you wait just a minute. You accusin' my boy of somethin'?" Pa's hands clenched into fists, and he raised his voice. "He ain't no liar."

Ma placed her arm around Chad's shoulder. She looked at him with pleading eyes and, in a stern voice, asked, "Chad, you ain't lying, are ya?"

"No, Ma. Honest. Cross my heart and hope to die." Chad crossed himself and looked at Ma with puppy-dog eyes. The lie stuck in his throat.

"Tom," Pa said, looking back at the red-faced old man. "What's goin' on here?"

Tom tightened his fists. "Your boy's been messin' with what belongs to me." Tom lurched toward Chad. "You best give it back right now, or I'll—"

"I didn't take nothin'," Chad sputtered.

"Now, wait a minute," Pa put his hand out to block Tom from getting any closer to Chad. "If he says he didn't take nothin', I believe him. You best leave now." Pa stood firm.

Tom spat on the ground and climbed back onto the wagon. He shot Chad a dirty look, snapped his whip, and gave a holler. The wagon took off in a dusty cloud.

The family stepped back into the cabin and sat down at the table. Chad stared down at his plate.

"You finish eating now," Ma said softly.

"Chad, you sure you don't know what he was talkin' about?"

Chad shook in fear. How could he have lied to his ma and pa? What would the pastor think if he found out? He shrugged and lowered his eyes, the lie eating him up inside. His stomach felt sick.

"Yes, Pa. I never took nothin' from him."

Pa scratched his head. "Well, maybe that ole cuss is loco. Let's just get back to eatin' and forget the whole thing."

Chad could not forget. He had never lied to Pa before. Maybe he had better stay far away from the cave—but could he?

Shame followed him around for days. He lost his appetite and could not sleep. At night, he tossed and turned, thinking about the evil son he had become. During the day, he fidgeted. If Ma and Pa discovered he lied, would they ever trust him again? What would Aubrey have to say about Tom's visit?

MISSING TREASURE

Several days later, Pastor Duell greeted Chad after the Sunday service at the Episcopal church.

"And how are you, Chad?" the pastor asked.

"Good, sir." He gave the pastor a puzzled look.

"Something bothering you, son?"

Chad thought for a moment. "Pastor, is it wrong to steal somethin' that somebody already stole?"

Pastor placed his hand on Chad's shoulder. He paused. "Well, I suppose not if you returned whatever was stolen to the owner."

"Thanks." Chad smiled and hurried over to Aubrey standing nearby.

"Aubrey, somebody took Tom's chest," Chad whispered in her ear. "We need to find out who and give it back to him. I don't think he's a thief, just an old codger. Whatever is in the chest must be very important to him. It's the right thing to do."

"I suppose you're right, or he wouldn't have gone to your house." Aubrey tightened her bonnet.

Junior appeared from the small group of people and strutted over to them. Chad's worry about Junior causing a problem loomed in his head. He had a feeling trouble was headed his way.

"Whatcha you two whisperin' about?" Junior sneered.

Chad stared Junior in the eyes. "Did you take the chest?"

"What chest?" He cocked his head questioningly.

"Stop actin' like you don't know." Chad got in Junior's face.

Junior backed off. "Have you gone loco? What you talkin' about?"

"You know. Don't lie." Chad puffed up in anger. He suddenly shoved Junior. "You give it back."

Pastor Duell rushed in between Chad and Junior and pushed them apart. "Boys, what are you arguing about? You just got out of Sunday service."

Junior glared at Chad. "He's gone loco, pastor."

"Chad, what's going on here?" Pastor Duell asked.

Chad, embarrassed, felt his face turn the color of an Indian paintbrush in full bloom. He bit his lip.

"Chad?" the pastor asked again.

"Sorry, Pastor. I can't say." Chad slumped and kicked at the ground.

"Well, I would appreciate it if you boys would stop whatever is happening. It is Sunday after all." The pastor shrugged and heaved a heavy sigh. "I think it would be best if you went home now."

Pastor waited until Junior had walked away before he left to visit some of the other church members.

When the pastor was out of sight, Junior turned around and cautiously approached Chad again.

"I didn't take it. I saw it in the cave, but I thought if Tom caught me…I'd be in a heap of trouble." Junior kicked at the dirt.

"If you didn't take it, then who did?" Chad looked confused.

Junior pointed to Aubrey. "Maybe *she* took it. You can't

trust Red Fox."

"How could you even say that?" Aubrey bristled. She placed her hands on her hips and stomped. Her face burned red in anger. She scowled at Junior like he was the devil himself.

"Aubrey didn't take it," Chad said reassuringly. "I know she didn't."

"Well, it sure weren't me," Junior said sharply and tromped off.

Chad and Aubrey decided they had to go back to the cave later that afternoon. They needed some evidence to help them solve the mystery of the stolen chest.

———— ♦ ————

Chad and Aubrey returned to the cave. They searched the area around the cave, making sure they were alone before entering the cave. Things looked the same except for an empty can of chew. The can could have been Tom's, but maybe, just maybe, it wasn't.

"Let's check around the outside of the cave. Might be footprints or somethin'," Chad said. He searched the brush and trees for any signs that might help him decide who or what had been there. The sun suddenly disappeared behind a cloud that cast a heavy, dark shadow over him. A distant rumble caught Chad's attention as he looked skyward. "Best be keepin' an eye out on the sky. Don't want to get caught in another storm."

"Me, either," Aubrey tightened her bonnet.

Chad and Aubrey checked behind downed trees and boulders for any more signs that might tell them who could have taken the chest. The wind picked up and rustled the leaves. The sky grew darker and ominous.

"Chad, look," Aubrey said excitedly. "The buffalo berry bush! A piece of red cloth!"

Chad examined the cloth. Where had he seen cloth like this before? He searched the ground around it.

"It's here, Aubrey! The chest is here!"

Somebody had tucked it into the end of a hollow log and probably left in a hurry. It had not yet been opened. Now, they had a chance to return it to the cave, but would Tom return to the cave and find the chest? Chad feared Tom wouldn't leave him alone.

An ominous flash of lightning and an instant crack of thunder made them jump. "That was close." Aubrey furrowed her brow.

"We'd better hurry." Chad clutched the chest tightly.

Chad and Aubrey rushed back to the entrance of the cave. Since it did not look like anyone was around, they entered. Chad placed the wooden chest where he had seen it the first time. Relieved, he stood back and studied the chest for a moment. What was in it? Had he done the right thing in returning it?

"Let's go before Tom finds us here." Chad turned to Aubrey and smiled. "I think we did the right thing."

Aubrey looked at the chest longingly. "I know, but it sure would have been nice to be rich."

Chad decided to tell Ma and Pa what really happened, no matter what the consequences. It would ease his mind, but he worried Ma and Pa would never trust him again.

Chad and Aubrey decided the next time they were in town, they would tell Tom the truth about what happened. Then, hopefully, Tom would forgive them.

On the way home, they hurried down the path along the creek. The wind tossed the tops of the trees and made them swirl. Birds and squirrels scattered ahead of them. They caught the smell of something burning. Black smoke filtered between the trees, and the sky darkened. They rushed through the trees and brush that slapped and scratched their faces until they burst into the meadow. A wall of flames raced toward them. The lightning had started the dry grasses afire. The wind fanned the flames in their direction. Heavy smoke and ash enveloped them, choking them with every breath.

Another bolt of lightning struck nearby, followed by a deafening boom.

"We can't go back through the meadow," Chad shouted through the dense smoke. "Head for the creek!"

Out of breath and afraid of burning alive, they raced to the edge of the creek and searched for a place that might provide some protection. On the other side of the water, the large boulders might be a haven from the flames—maybe their only hope of survival.

Chad and Aubrey's eyes teared from the acrid smoke. Coughing hard, they splashed and fumbled through the knee-deep water to the other side of the creek. Gray ash and bits of burning twigs and leaves covered them. Smoke engulfed everything. Chad helped Aubrey nestle into the narrow crevice of some granite boulders. He hoped to protect her there.

"What if the trees catch fire?" Aubrey screamed. She grabbed Chad's arm tightly. "I don't want to die like my Pa or be scarred like Ma. Help me! Help me!"

"Take off your apron. We'll use it to cover our heads."

Hot billowing smoke and flames blew through the trees and across the water. They were at the mercy of the wind. The fire's heat threatened to bake them alive. Chad and Aubrey gasped for air. Would the boulders keep them safe? Would they die from the flames or suffocate from the smoke?

Another deadly streak of lightning made a deafening boom resonate against the mountains. The roar of the fire grew louder. Suddenly, a blast of freezing air howled through the forest with such force that everything—trees, plants, and wildlife—bowed to its fury. A cloudburst of rain unleashed. Drenched and shivering, they desperately tried to crawl deeper into the shelter of the boulders. Torrential rain continued to batter them. Aubrey sobbed. Chad tried to protect her with his body, but he was so paralyzed with fear that he could hardly breathe. When would the nightmare end?

After what seemed like forever, the rain turned into a light sprinkle. Chad poked his head out from the boulder. The wind stopped abruptly; the smoke cleared.

"Aubrey, the fire is out!" Chad smiled strong and wide.

"No, Chad! Look! The creek is all muddy and rising fast," Aubrey shouted.

"Flash flood! Get to higher ground. Quick!"

Slipping and sliding on the wet boulders, Chad and Aubrey scrambled as high as they could. In a moment, a torrent of dirty water swollen with debris barreled down the creek. Logs, branches, and a dead deer careened by them.

"No! It can't be happening again! No!" Aubrey screamed above the roaring water.

"I know. Second time this year," Chad said.

The flood only lasted a short time, but Chad shook until it ended. Nature could turn without warning. Who knew what tomorrow would bring?

FATAL

Several weeks passed before Chad and Aubrey went into town again. Hints of the changing season were beginning to show up everywhere. The chokecherries had been picked, and the bushes had turned crimson. The cottonwoods along the creek sported gold leaves among their crowns. The days were warm, but the nights cooler. Frost had already killed the sunflowers. Pa butchered the fattened hog for winter, and Ma harvested a fine crop of potatoes with Chad's help.

When the first day of school arrived, Chad ate lunch with Aubrey at recess. Chad had just opened his lard pail to have a bite of cornbread with molasses when Brett walked over to him and sat down.

"Howdy, Brett," Aubrey said.

"Howdy."

"You got somethin' on your mind?" Chad asked.

"Nope, just thought I'd sit and visit a while."

Chad thought it unusual for Brett just to come up and join him and Aubrey for lunch. Brett did not usually say very much. "How come you're not eatin' with Junior?"

Brett just shrugged. Chad thought that was strange. He took another bite of his cornbread. In the back of his mind, he knew something wasn't right.

"What happened to your bandana?" Aubrey eyed him with suspicion. "You've got a big tear in it."

Brett fidgeted. He had a guilty look on his face. "I...I don't know."

Chad looked up at Brett and his bandana—the red bandana he always wore. The same red material, like the piece Aubrey noticed caught on a branch by the cave.

"You! *You* took the chest," Chad said in a hushed but accusatory voice.

Brett's eyes grew wide. His hands shook, so he stood up and faced Chad.

"I didn't want to take it, but Junior made me go back and get it." Brett swallowed hard. "And then Wildcat Tom was comin' up the trail, so I hid it in the log." Tears welled up in his eyes. "You won't tell nobody, will ya?"

Chad thought for a moment. Anger sizzled inside him because Tom blamed him for taking the chest, but he felt sorry for Brett, too. He knew what a bully Junior could be.

"I won't tell on ya. Besides, Aubrey and me found it. We took it back to the cave."

"You did?" Brett looked relieved. "I ain't never stole nothin' before, and I won't ever do that again."

Chad set his lunch down and stood. He hustled over to where Junior sat, eating his lunch alone. Aubrey followed him.

"Junior, you're a scoundrel!"

"What you talkin' about?" Junior stood and looked down at Chad.

"You know darn well what I'm talkin' about." Chad clenched his fists. "You made Brett go back to the cave and steal the chest."

Junior backed off. "Maybe I did, or I didn't, but I ain't got no chest."

Chad's face turned red, and he shook with anger. "No wonder Brett ain't eatin' lunch with you. What kind of friend makes somebody try to steal for him?"

Junior smirked. "Well, you and your girlfriend were gonna steal the chest."

Chad just shook his head and turned away. He knew Junior was right. At first, he and Aubrey were going to steal the chest, but his conscience would not let him. Aubrey agreed.

He wanted Wildcat Tom to know that he had not taken the chest but that he had found it and returned it.

The next day, Chad and Aubrey found themselves in town again. The hot day made Chad sweat, but his tongue felt as dry as the Powder River that time of year. The thought of speaking to Tom frightened him. Chad now had a chance to tell him what had really happened. He discovered that Tom lived in a small cabin by Clear Creek at the end of town. Chad and Aubrey approached the weathered cabin with the sod roof with caution. The snarl and bared teeth of the wolf scared them. Tom had left his wolf, Granite, chained to a small cottonwood tree near the cabin. The deep growl made them even more nervous.

Chad's hands shook at the thought of confronting Tom, but he knocked on the door anyway. He stepped back, half expecting Tom to burst through the door in a rage. Nobody answered. He tried again. And again.

"Guess he's not home. Let's go," Chad said. In a way, he was glad, almost relieved, but deep inside, he knew the right thing to do was to tell Tom. "Guess we come back another time."

Chad feared the wolf yet was fascinated. Bigger than any dog he had ever seen, the wolf had thick silver-gray fur, its deep dark eyes seemed full of mystery. The wolf paced menacingly and eyed Chad. He noticed the wolf panting from the heat. Its water bowl was dry. Chad was not quite sure why, but he felt sorry for the animal. He carefully reached for the bowl to fetch it some water from the creek.

"Be careful, Chad." Aubrey stepped back as she warned him.

Granite snarled the second Chad reached for the bowl—the animal lurched out. Chad was too close. The wolf pounced and knocked him to the ground. It caught his arm. Chad tried to fight it off. He kicked and tried to pull away, but then it lashed out at his leg. Terror gripped him in a vice of extreme pain. He screamed, knowing he could be mauled to death.

"Aubrey! Aubrey! Run! Get help!"

Aubrey froze for a moment at the sight of such horror.

"Aubrey! Help!"

Adrenaline kicked in, and Aubrey raced toward the street. "Help! Help! The wolf's tearing Chad apart. It's gonna kill him!"

Some townsfolk heard her cries and scrambled toward Tom's cabin. Thankfully, Sheriff Mitchell heard her screams, too. He sped across Main Street, carrying his rifle.

By the time he reached Chad, the wolf was tossing him around like a rag doll. The sheriff could not shoot until he had a clean shot.

Chad screamed, begging the sheriff to shoot, but the wolf had him and shook him so violently the sheriff could not shoot.

When the sheriff finally had a clear shot, he aimed. A bullet to the head killed the attacking animal. Chad collapsed into a bloody heap.

"Quick!" Sheriff Mitchell said to another man standing nearby. "Help me get him to Doc Johnson's place."

Chad could not see because of the blood in his eyes. Shock took hold—he could not feel any pain. Half in and out of consciousness, Chad thought he heard Aubrey screaming and crying. Or was it a dream? A nightmarish dream? He forced himself to focus on the situation. What had just happened to him? Why was he being carried away? What would Ma and Pa say? And then everything went blank.

Doc Johnson was out on a ranch visit, so Chad was rushed to Fort McKinney by the military ambulance. Chad needed to see Dr. Lott, the post-surgeon.

Through blurry eyes, he saw Ma and Pa standing by his bedside.

"What happened?" Chad squinted. "Where am I?"

"Tom's wolf attacked you," Pa said.

Ma sniffled. "It almost killed you."

Then, it all came back. He remembered picking up the bowl to get Granite some water. His stomach felt queasy. When he moved, his arm and leg hurt, and his head ached. How could this have happened?

BETTER THAN GOLD

It had been a week since the wolf attack, and Chad was still hurt. Doc Johnson said he was lucky to be alive and that Doctor Lott had done a fine job of stitching him back together. He insisted Chad stay in bed and rest so he could heal. Chad had lost a lot of blood. His left ear had been torn off, and a nasty gash crossed his cheek. His arm had fifty-seven stitches. The pain in his leg hurt the worst. The thought of having only one ear bothered him, yet he could still hear. Why did he get so close to the wolf? He should have known better.

Ma and Pa were not pleased that he and Aubrey had kept the Ice Cave and the chest a secret. Chad wished he had told them. Why had he let his curiosity get the better of him?

Ma fussed over him so much that he felt bad. He could not do his chores to help her. Pa did not say much, but the sadness in his face spoke more than words. When Aubrey came to visit the first time, she gasped at the sight of him and then cried. Miss Bryant visited and brought him a book to read. She let a tear slip and left abruptly. Pastor Duell stopped by and let Chad know he was grateful he was alive and would pray for a fast recovery.

Aubrey had told Sheriff Mitchell why Chad had stopped by Tom's cabin. When Wildcat Tom returned to town from his trapping on the mountain, Sheriff Mitchell explained everything to him.

———◆———

One afternoon, Chad heard a wagon pull up to the cabin. Much to his surprise, it was Wildcat Tom. He knocked on the cabin door.

"May I come in?" Tom removed his dirty hat.

Pa opened the door cautiously, and Tom entered.

"I'm afraid I owe you and your boy an apology," Tom said. "Chad didn't take nothin' from me. As a matter of fact, he was returning somethin' most valuable to me."

"He's in here," Pa said.

Ma patted the bun on the top of her head, clasped her hands, and gave him a stern nod. She had blamed Tom for Chad's accident and could not seem to forgive him.

"Chad, I come to make peace with ya," Tom said as he sheepishly stepped into the bedroom. Tom stared at Chad's stitched head and face. "Sheriff Mitchell told me the whole story. I know ya didn't take my chest."

Chad groaned uncomfortably and sat up in his bed. "I'm sorry I caused you so much trouble."

"That don't matter none now," Tom said. "But I thought you should know what was in my chest. I'm no outlaw, and it weren't no gold in the chest." Chad stared at the old man. He did not look so scary now; it was as if the meanness had left him like a thundercloud after the storm.

"Why did you keep it in the cave?" Chad asked.

"I'm on the trail a lot. Thought it would be safe there." Tom sighed. "It was all the things from my past that brought me comfort." Tom paused. "Ya see, I once had a wife and a son. They died from the fever." Tom looked down at the floor and then up again at Chad. "Sometimes memories is worth more than gold. That chest held my wife's wedding ring, Bible, pictures, and…this."

Tom reached into his pocket, pulled out a gold watch on a chain, and handed it to Chad. "I was goin' to give this to my son, Jedidiah, when he growed to be a man, but…anyway, I'd like you to have it." He swallowed really hard. "I'm sorry for what Granite did to ya."

Chad rubbed the smooth surface of the gold watch. He didn't know what to say. He thought for a moment.

"Thank you. I be mighty pleased to have it."

Tom gave a weak smile, put on his hat, turned, and left without saying another word.

———◆———

Several weeks passed before Chad could visit the Foster place, but Aubrey had visited Chad as often as she could. She'd grown used to the scars left on Chad's face and arms, but although Mrs. Foster had sent get well wishes and fresh pumpkin pie, she had not yet seen Chad.

When Mrs. Foster saw Chad's scarred face, she gasped and placed her hands over her mouth. She collapsed into her rocker. Her whole body trembled. She stared at him. "Oh, Chad. I feel your pain."

"It's okay, Mrs. Foster. Now, I understand how you feel."

"I'm so grateful you're alive." She sighed. "Chad, remember it's not what you look like that counts. You have a big heart. That's more important than anything."

Aubrey reached out and held her ma's hand.

"I'm so sorry, Chad. Aubrey told me the whole story. You did the right thing in returning Wildcat Tom's chest."

"Thought it would be best."

"Chad, look who came to see you," Aubrey said.

Chad reached down to pick up Sunny. "You sure are gettin' to be a big boy."

"He's turning into a good mouser," Mrs. Foster said. She clasped her hands. "How's your ma?"

"Ma's fine. She's excited about the baby comin'. Me, too." Chad smiled. "I'm gonna be a big brother again."

Mrs. Foster nodded. "And you'll be a good one."

CONVERSATION WITH THE AUTHOR

1. Where did you get the idea for the Ice Cave Mystery?
The *Ice Cave Mystery* is a result of having hiked to a local site called the Ice Cave. It is just an opening in a rock slide at the base of a mountain, but you can climb into it and see stalagmite and stalactite ice formations at certain times of the year. I wanted to write a sequel to my book *Secret of the Black Widow* and chose it to be the focal point of my story.

2. How did you decide to have a character named Wildcat Tom?
I saw a photo in the Gatchell Museum in Buffalo, Wyoming, of an old *wolfer* called Wild Cat Tom, with a pet wolf and a coyote. He lived in 1890 (the exact time my story took place). I always knew that I wanted to write a story about him and so he became a character in the *Ice Cave Mystery*.

3. How do you begin to write your middle grade fiction books?
When I get the idea for a book, I start by trying to state the main idea of the story in a sentence. Then I make a simple outline of ten to twelve chapters, and go back and write what could happen in each chapter. I keep it flexible because I never follow it exactly.

4. What is your favorite book you have written?
Hard to say, but my adult poetry book *A Wyoming State of Mind* is special to me because it is a hard cover with colorful photos and says a lot about who I am, how I feel, and what I believe.

TOPICS AND QUESTIONS FOR *ICE CAVE MYSTERY*

1. When did Chad get the idea to find the Ice Cave?
2. Why didn't he want to tell Aubrey?
3. What made living in 1890 dangerous?
4. Where did Chad and Aubrey first see Wildcat Tom?
5. How did Chad know he was getting close to the cave?
6. Do you think the bats would have harmed them?
7. Should Chad and Aubrey have told their parents about the cave?
8. Why do you think Wildcat Tom had a pet wolf if he was a wolfer?
9. Do you think Wildcat Tom's treasure chest held something more valuable than gold?
10. What would you have done if you found a chest of gold?

THE REAL ICE CAVE

When I first heard about the Ice Cave from local people, after moving to Buffalo, Wyoming, I knew that I had to check it out. When I did find it, I was a bit disappointed. It was not a big cave as I had hoped. It was a large opening inside a landslide of boulders at the base of a mountain. I was able to crawl inside and stand upright in one place, but you could only crawl to one side or the other. It did have stalactites and stalagmites of ice in early spring. However, I knew it would make a great story someday if I imagined it bigger.

ACKNOWLEGMENT

I would like to acknowledge Nancy Tabb for all her help in my research for the Ice Cave Mystery.

I would also like to acknowledge Deanna Estes for all my wonderful book covers.

ABOUT THE AUTHOR

Known by many as the "teacher who dances on his desk," Eugene M. Gagliano (pronounced Galiano) is a retired elementary teacher with a great sense of humor. He is a graduate of the Institute of Children's Literature. Gagliano and his wife Carol, who have four children and seven grandchildren, live near the Big Horn Mountains in Wyoming with their two cats, Sitsi and Buster, and a purebred chow, Ruby. He enjoys reading and writing, traveling, hiking, acrylic painting, singing tenor in the community choir, and spending hours flower and vegetable gardening.

Email: **eugene.gagliano@gmail.com**
Website: **www.gargene.com**
FB Author Page: **www.facebook.com/dancingteacher**
Author Page on Amazon: **Amazon.com/author/www.gargene.com**

Turn the page for a preview of Eugene M. Gagliano's new novel.

Turn the page for a preview of
Eugene McBaglione's new novel.

RED FOX

The scream from the direction of the widow Foster's cabin made the hair rise on the back of Chad's neck.

"Scared?" James Junior asked.

"No, I just don't think it's right. She ain't never bothered me none," Chad said, but in his heart, he knew the truth. He was afraid.

"My dad says she's evil," Brett added.

"Afraid she might do somethin' to ya, Chad?" Junior teased.

"I told you, I just don't think it's right." Chad looked at his dusty boots. "Come on, we're goin' to be late for school."

The late April sunshine shone over the prairie, lighting the widow Foster's shabby pioneer cabin. As Chad and the other two boys approached the curve in the rutted wagon trail, a faint plume of ashen gray smoke rose from the stone chimney.

"Maybe she's waitin' for Chad to stop by," James said.

"Maybe—"

"Look," Brett interrupted. "There's the Black Widow now."

Chad felt uneasy. He pushed his straw hat down tight on his head. The widow, wearing a black dress, appeared in front of the log cabin which stood about fifty yards from the trail. A slight breeze tugged at her bonnet as she glided toward the well. Chad figured either she didn't see him or the other boys, or she pretended not to.

"Can you see it?" Junior asked.

"No. She's too far away," Brett answered.

Chad watched the widow lower her bucket into the well. He shifted his gaze back to the cabin. A little boy stood staring in the doorway. His bleached-white hair glowing in the sunlight made him look like a straw doll. A girl stepped out of the doorway and kissed the boy's cheek. Chad knew her name—Aubrey Foster. She was eleven, one year younger than he was. He watched Aubrey grab a worn woolen shawl from a hook by the door.

"Bye, Mama," Aubrey said, shaking her fiery-red braids. Her mother mumbled something without looking up.

"Here comes the Red Fox," Junior chuckled. "Maybe Chad could ask her what her mother's hidin'."

Like everyone else, Chad wondered why the widow always wore a black veil when she went to town. Why did she always turn away from people and speak softly like a light breeze? Nobody knew much about her. Why did it seem so important to see her face up close without the veil? Chad knew it was none of his business anyway.

Aubrey made her way up the trail a little before Junior and Brett caught up to her. Chad deliberately stayed back a way.

"Hey, Red Fox," Junior said. "Got any new freckles?"

Aubrey kept walking. She clenched her fist and ignored Junior. Junior reached up behind her and pulled at her braid.

"Ouch!" Aubrey turned and glared at Junior. "Leave me alone or I'll—"

"Or you'll what?"

Aubrey stomped her foot. Her face tightened. She turned and hurried up the trail toward the Chokecherry Creek schoolhouse. Junior and Brett walked faster to catch up with her.

Chad wished there were other boys his age to be friends with besides Junior and Brett.

"Leave her alone." Chad kicked at a stone in the trail.

"What did you say?" Junior gave Chad a mean look.

"Leave her alone so we can go to the creek. I saw some big fish in the bend yesterday."

"I s'pose," Junior said.

Chad took off at full speed. "Last one to the creek is a rotten egg." Junior stood tall for a 12-year-old, but Chad ran faster.

The water in the bend flowed smooth and deep. Chad and the other boys slapped ripples into the icy water with their hands as shadowy fish darted beneath the water. A cool breeze rustled the tattered grasses left from last summer. Chad breathed the earthy smell of spring. He heard the clang of the school bell and sighed. He wished he could watch the creek all morning.

When Chad reached the log schoolhouse, his teacher, Miss Maple Bryant, greeted the boys with a stern look.

"You three were almost late again. Got a touch of spring fever?" Her pinched lips melted into a smile. "Come on in. We have work to do."

"Yes, ma'am." Chad hurried in. Chad liked Miss Bryant, and he thought she liked him, too. Miss Bryant made the children work hard, but she was fair. Chad liked her reddish-brown hair tied neatly into a bun. Miss Bryant wore plain calico, high-collared dresses, and she smelled sweet and clean. Chad thought she looked like a prairie meadow in bloom.

The chilly morning air left the one-room schoolhouse once the heat from the small, black wood stove filled the room. The rough wooden bench made sitting difficult as Chad stared blankly at his slate board. A meadowlark's sweet song pulled his attention toward the window. He could see down the trail, and his thoughts turned to the widow. He wondered whether she really was evil. If she was, then he surely had good reason to be afraid of her.

Made in the USA
Las Vegas, NV
10 September 2024